For Ma & Pa

THIS IS A BORZOI BOOK PUBLISHED BY ALFRED A. KNOPF

Copyright © 2009 by Hannah Shaw

All rights reserved. Published in the United States by
Alfred A. Knopf, an imprint of Random House Children's Books,
a division of Random House, Inc., New York.
Originally published in Great Britain in 2009 by Jonathan Cape,
an imprint of Random House Children's Books.

Knopf, Borzoi Books, and the colophon are registered
trademarks of Random House, Inc.

Visit us on the Web! www.randomhouse.com/kids

Educators and librarians, for a variety of teaching tools, visit us at
www.randomhouse.com/teachers

Library of Congress Cataloging-in-Publication Data is available upon request.
ISBN: 978-0-375-86105-5 (trade) – ISBN: 978-0-375-96105-2 (lib. bdg.)

MANUFACTURED IN MALAYSIA
February 2010
10 9 8 7 6 5 4 3 2 1
First American Edition

Random House Children's Books
supports the First Amendment
and celebrates the right to read.

The nicest Nutti Nutts!

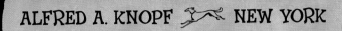

ALFRED A. KNOPF • NEW YORK

ERROLL

by
Hannah Shaw

One day, Bob found a squirrel in his package of nuts.

"Yikes!" yelled Bob.

"Crikes!" squeaked the squirrel.

Squirrels didn't usually talk, so Bob was sure that this one must be rather *special.*

"**I'm Bob,**" said Bob.
"**What's your name?**"

"**I'm Erroll,**" said Erroll.

START HERE

Nutt
Nutt

Nu

NUT COLLECT
CONTROL

N N N

Nut
Nu

N

N N N

N

A
GOOD
OF
NUT

Bob could only imagine how
Erroll had gotten inside
the package of nuts in the
first place. . . .

"You must be hungry after all that," said Bob.

So he made Erroll a peanut butter sandwich.
And another . . . and another. . . .

"I like peanut butter, too," said Bob.

Erroll **stuffed** his face, spraying crumbs everywhere.

Soon he was covered from **head to tail** in peanut butter.

"You need a bath!" said Bob.
But Erroll didn't like water.

"It's got bubbles," said Bob.
But Erroll didn't
like bubbles, either.

So Bob tried cleaning Erroll
with his mom's toothbrush . . .

FRESH MINT

but Erroll wasn't fond
of that plan. . . .

He *ran,* **jumped,** and
climbed all over.

Finally, Bob cornered him.

A trail of
dirty
paw
prints

led Bob all the way to the top
of Mom's favorite curtains,
where Erroll was
swinging
dangerously.

Erroll scrambled up
the tree as quick as a flash.
He sat at the top waiting
for Bob.

"It's a very long way down,"
said Bob, trying not to sound scared.

"Oh no, I'm stuck," he wailed
a few moments later.

Luckily, Erroll was there
to help him climb down safely.

"Look at this mess! What have you been doing?" said Bob's mom.

"Erroll did it," said Bob.

"*Who* is Erroll?" she asked.

"He's the talking squirrel I found in my package of nuts," Bob explained.

"There's no such thing as a talking . . ."

"How do you do?"
said Erroll.

"Aaaaaaack!"

cried Bob's mom.

Bob told his mom everything.

When she had
calmed down,
she said that Erroll
would have to go
back home.

"Not back in the package!"
said Bob in dismay.

"No, back to the woods!"
said his mom.

Bob was sad that Erroll
was going home,
even if he *had* gotten him
into lots of trouble.

He made Erroll a
triple mega
peanut butter
sandwich
as a goodbye
present.

"Goodbye, Erroll," said Bob.
And when his mom wasn't looking,
he whispered,
"Come back
and visit
me soon!"

"Bye-bye, Bob,"
said Erroll.

Erroll's friends were extremely
pleased to see him again.

He told them all about his
adventures with his new friend Bob.

Nut-Store

The next day, Bob had **Chewy Crunchy Monkey Munchy** for breakfast. . . .

ERROLL

TLY NEWS

SQUIRRELS
INVADE
NUT FACTORY
"THEY WERE
LOOKING FOR
PEANUT BUTTER"

NUTTI NUT
FACTO
IN

Can *you* guess what happened next?